My Horse of the North

written and photo-illustrated by Bruce McMillan

SCHOLASTIC PRESS ✦ NEW YORK

Fyrir Lori
að eilífu

This book was made possible
with the generous help and assistance of:
Einar Gustavsson, the Iceland Tourist Bureau;
Debbie Scott and Margrét Hauksdóttir, Icelandair;
Þórunn Reynisdóttir, Icelandair/Hertz Car Rental;
Vigfús Vigfússon, Hótel Áning, Sauðárkrókur and Varmahlið, and
Lovísa "Lolla" Birna Björnsdóttir, Margrét Vigfúsdóttir's parents;
Álfhildur Leifsdóttir, Sölvi Sigurðarson, Leifur Þórarinsson,
Kristín Ólafsdóttir, and Ögri, the horse, Keldudalur Farm in Hegranes;
Ingimar Pálsson and Perla, the horse; Lori Evans, equestrian advisor;
and the children in order of appearance: Margrét Guðny Vigfúsdóttir,
Kristín Schiöth Alfreðsdóttir, and Axel Aage Schiöth Alfreðson.

Library of Congress Cataloging-in-Publication Data

McMillan, Bruce
My horse of the North / Bruce McMillan.   p. cm.
Summary: Describes how a young girl living fifty miles from the
Arctic Circle gets her horse ready to participate in the annual réttir,
or gathering of sheep, in their farming community in Iceland.
ISBN 0-590-97205-7
1. Iceland horse—Juvenile literature. 2. Horses—Iceland—Juvenile literature.
3. Shepherds—Juvenile literature. 4. Farm life—Iceland—Juvenile literature.
5. Iceland—Social life and customs—Juvenile literature. [1. Farm life—Iceland.
2. Iceland horse. 3. Horses. 4. Iceland—Social life and customs.]   I. Title
SF315.2.I3M36   1997   636.3' 145'09412—dc21   96-45241   CIP   AC

10 9 8 7 6 5 4 3 2 1

Printed in Singapore   46
First edition, September 1997

Design and typesetting by Bruce McMillan
All type was set in Palatino. Text type was set in 18 point.

Iceland

These photos were taken during the summer of 1996. They show an area in northern Iceland, Skagafjörður (*SKAH·gah·fyor·thur*), fifty miles south (eighty kilometers) of the Arctic Circle. Patches of ice and small glaciers remain in the hills all summer. At the center of this area is the second-largest town in northern Iceland, Sauðárkrókur (*SAU·thar·krok·ur*). It has a population of about 2,800.

In the north there are no naturally growing trees. Driftwood washes in across the Arctic Ocean and Norwegian Sea from Siberia. It's often used as fence posts on farms. Skagafjörður is known for its farms. Sheep are raised in great numbers for their wool and meat. But this area is especially known for its horse-breeding farms. They raise the small, but strong and hardy, "Icelandic horse" breed. By law, no other breed has been allowed into Iceland for almost 1,000 years.

The photos were taken—often on very breezy days—using a Nikon F4/MF23 with 24, 85, 105 micro, 180, and 300 mm lenses, usually with a polarizing filter when shooting in full sunlight. The 35 mm film, Kodachrome 64, was processed by Kodak in Fair Lawn, New Jersey.

Summer
Northern Iceland

Lambs and their mothers roam freely in the mountains all summer. They wander among patches of ice. They feed on wild plants and grasses. Their wool coats grow long.

In the valley below, Margrét (*MAR·grree·yet*) looks up to the hills. She can only dream of what's to come at summer's end. Will she and her new horse be ready for réttir (*RRYET·ir*)?

5

Margrét leads her horse to the pasture. "Minn hestur" (*MIN HEST·oorr*), she says fondly, which means "my horse," in Icelandic.

Perla (*PERR·la*) is twelve—three years older than Margrét. She is small, yet strong. Her color is chestnut brown with dapples that spot her coat. She has a thick gold mane, a gold tail, and a stripe down her nose with a snip at the tip.

Perla is an "Icelandic horse," a gentle, friendly breed unique to Iceland. Her ancestors arrived with the Vikings over a thousand years ago.

Margrét's favorite farm chore is grooming Perla. As she brushes Perla's coat, Margrét whispers, "Réttir. Réttir. Réttir." Perla's ears prick up, and she nuzzles her new owner.

Margrét and Perla will ride in their first réttir at the end of summer. So will Margrét's friends, Kristín and Axel, and Perla's stable mate, Ögri (OO·rree). But, first, they must practice.

At milking time Margrét gets an idea. Today they won't walk the cows to the barn. They will herd them in with Perla and Ögri.

The horses respond well, but cows are too easy to herd. The cows know the way and just plod along. She and Perla need to practice with animals that are harder to herd.

One morning while riding, Margrét has another idea. "Gæser!" (GUYZ·eerr), she calls out to her friends. That means "geese!" Axel and Kristín just laugh. Herding geese on horseback? There are more than a hundred geese here on Keldudalur (KEL·doo·dah·luhr) Farm. It won't be as easy as herding cows.

Margrét eyes the flock. She and Perla must work together. They approach the geese. The geese eye them back. Then they honk and flap as they waddle off in all directions.

Margrét guides Perla with her voice, a squeeze of her legs, and a gentle tug on the reins. Perla responds, and they circle the geese. Once gathered, the geese parade to the river, followed by a proud Margrét and Perla.

"Góður hestur" (GOTH·oorr HEST·oorr), says Margrét, which means "good horse." They are becoming a working team here in the north of Iceland.

Summer days are sometimes warm, and Margrét rides without a sweater.

But most days are cool. On those days, she wears a hand-knit woolen sweater. Margrét's sweater fits her now, but she is growing. Her mother will knit her a new one—if Margrét and Perla help bring home the wool before winter.

All summer the children work with their horses. They practice riding. Sometimes they trot. Sometimes they gallop as fast as they can.

By late summer the children are skilled riders. Finally, Margrét and Perla are ready to try herding some of the fastest animals on the farm.

They herd the rams—the male sheep. Like the geese, the rams try to run in all directions. But Margrét and Perla know what to do. Margrét yells out, "Já! Já!" *(YOW YOW)*, which means "yes! yes!" as she urges Perla on. They herd the group from field to field.

Now Margrét and Perla are ready— and just in time.

It's September. The fífa (FEE·vah), the "cotton grass," that they ride through, has gone to seed. It's time for réttir—the big roundup. It's time to bring the rest of the sheep home.

Winter in Iceland is long, cold, and dark. The lambs and ewes must return to their farms for food and shelter.

On the day of réttir, it rains. The wind is cold. Margrét and Perla, and their neighbors, leave for the mountains at dawn.

When she and Perla cross the ridge, Margrét gasps. There are so many sheep! But Margrét is ready. Perla is ready. Their friends are ready. The grown lambs and their mothers are ready, too. All around Iceland, it's time to herd the sheep home from the mountains. And herd they do!

Margrét and Perla are right behind the sheep. Their practice has paid off. Margrét yells out "Hó! Hó!" (*HAUH HAUH*), to move them along. As the sheep run down the valley, they bleat back, *baa, baa*. The sounds of calling and bleating echo between the mountains.

There are young sheep and old sheep. There are black sheep. There are white sheep. There are even black-and-white sheep. And on this rainy day they are all soggy sheep.

Some of the sheep stray. Perla's mane blows in the breeze as Margrét guides them back to the flock. She and Perla, with Ögri and his rider alongside, herd them down the valley.

Along the journey, the sheep try to stop and eat. Margrét and Perla urge them on. All of the animals can eat when they are down from the mountains. And they do.

29

Margrét thanks Perla. Now there will be wool for Margrét's mother to knit her a new sweater.

Margrét and her friends hug. "Við Gerðum það!" (*VIDTH GER·thum THOTH*), they cheer, which means "we did it!"

About Iceland's Réttir

In the winter sheep live in barns. But in the spring, after the lambs are born, both ewes and their lambs are set free in the mountains. All summer over a million sheep graze in Iceland's mountains. That is more than four times the human population of this island country. The Icelandic sheep are an ancient Nordic breed with short tails, and, usually, a white coat.

In September, a certain day is set aside in each farming community for réttir—the sheep roundup—in the surrounding mountains. The sure-footed Icelandic horse, a breed that dates back to the ninth century, is adept at climbing over rocky terrain. This is the same breed brought to Iceland by the Vikings. They carry twice as much weight as other horses, yet survive on only one-third of the food. There are 60-70,000 of these smooth-riding, small horses in Iceland—about one for every four people. By law, dating back almost a thousand years, no other breeds are allowed to enter Iceland. Not only does the breed stay pure, but there is also little chance of importing communicable disease.

In the pre-dawn dark, experienced riders mount their horses and leave for the highlands. They herd the sheep to the lowlands, and then to a réttir pen. It's a circular pen, with a central area for sorting the animals, literally the hub of activity. Each farm family guides their sheep into separate stalls that radiate off the central area. In rural areas, such as the one depicted in this book, réttir is a social event, and guests are welcome. At day's end there is much celebrating. In some areas it has become a major end-of-summer social event, and sometimes there are more people than sheep. They celebrate into the night. Even after a long, hard day's work, the Icelandic people know how to have a good time.

It's possible to ride Icelandic horses without going to Iceland. There are more than 1,000 horses in the United States. For information on the location of Icelandic horse farms in North America contact the United States Icelandic Horse Congress, 38 Park St., Montclair, NJ 07042.

Experienced riders who would like to help at an Icelandic sheep réttir, or go on an organized trek through the wild areas of Iceland on an Icelandic horse, may get more information from The Icelandic Tourist Board, 655 Third Avenue, New York, NY 10017.

For information about sweaters made from the wool of Iceland's free ranging sheep contact The Handknitting Association of Iceland, Skólavöðstig #19, Reykjavík, Iceland.

Bibliography

Carwardine, Mark. *Iceland, Nature's Meeting Place: A Wildlife Guide.* Reykjavík: Iceland Review, 1986.

Glendening, P.J.T. *Teach Yourself Icelandic.* London: NTC Publishing Group, 1961.

Ingimarsson, Ingimar, and Gísli Pálsson. *Horses of the North.* Iceland: Bókaútgáfan á Hofi, 1992.

Kristinsson, Hörður. *A Guide to the Flowering Plants and Ferns of Iceland.* Iceland: Örn og Örlygur Publishing House, 1987.

Magnússon, Sigurður. *The Natural Colors of the Icelandic Horse.* Reykjavík: Mál og menning, 1996.

Thórarinsson, Örn, ed. *Guide to Skagafjörður and Siglufjörður.* Iceland: Bóka og blaðaútgáfa Arnar, 1993.

Keldudalur Farm, Hegranes, Iceland